This Little Tiger book belongs to:

_____

_____

_____

For Lucy and Ruben, with love
— D.H.
For Tim and Noah
— J.C.

LITTLE TIGER PRESS LTD,
an imprint of the Little Tiger Group
1 Coda Studios, 189 Munster Road,
London SW6 6AW
www.littletiger.co.uk

First published in Great Britain 2001
This edition published 2017

The Very Busy Day

by
Diana Hendry

Illustrated by
Jane Chapman

LITTLE TIGER
LONDON

It was a hot sunny day, and Big
Mouse was digging in the garden.

SWISH!

Little Mouse sat on the swing, wearing his sun hat. "There's a lot of digging to do," said Big Mouse. "Come and help me, Little Mouse." "I'm too busy to help," said Little Mouse. "I'm dreaming up something." And he swung up and down, up and down.

"You could put in these seeds," said Big Mouse. "If you plant them in the dark, they'll dream up flowers."

SWISH!

"Umm," said Little Mouse.
"But I've got my own dream,
and I'm busy thinking about it."
"Busy doing nothing,"
grumbled Big Mouse.

WHEEE!

Little Mouse slid off the swing and jumped into the wheelbarrow. He lay and gazed at the sky. "I need that wheelbarrow for the weeds," said Big Mouse. "And look at all the mess you've made."

Big Mouse tipped Little Mouse out onto the grass. "Please, Little Mouse, I need some help."
"I'm far too busy to help," cried Little Mouse, and he ran off to pick some daisies.

Big Mouse picked up all the
weeds. He mopped his brow
and rubbed his back.
"Phew, it's hot," he puffed . . .

"And this barrow's very heavy
all of a sudden."
It was heavy because Little
Mouse had jumped back in!
He was sitting on top of
the weeds making a
daisy chain.

"I'm not pushing you and the weeds," said Big Mouse indignantly. "Out you get! Come and help me take the weeds to the dump."
Little Mouse hung the daisy chain around his neck and scrambled out of the wheelbarrow.

But he didn't help
Big Mouse. He picked
lots and lots of clover
instead. He put the
clover in a flowerpot
on the back doorstep.

HUFF!
PUFF!

Big Mouse pushed the wheelbarrow to
the dump by himself, muttering crossly.

Big Mouse went to find his rake.
He couldn't see Little Mouse anywhere.
"Come on, Little Mouse," he called.
"There's a little rake here for you too."

As Big Mouse climbed down the ladder, Little Mouse poked his head out. "Can't you see I'm busy?" he called. "I'm collecting birds' feathers. This dream is very hard work." "Humph!" said Big Mouse. "There's dreaming and there's doing. What about a little doing from you!"

HUMPH!

Little Mouse had found
three snowy white feathers.
He laid them carefully
on the doorstep.
By now, Big Mouse
was busy.

"Little Mouse," he called. "You could help me carry this strawberry down the ladder." "Can't stop now," said Little Mouse. "I need something from the kitchen."

The sun had made Big
Mouse's head ache, and he
felt very peeved with Little
Mouse for not helping him.
"Whatever's he doing now?"
he grumbled.

Little Mouse rushed out into the garden. "Big Mouse, Big Mouse," he called. "Look what I've made for you!"

"It's your very own special sun hat!"
"Oh thank you, Little Mouse," said
Big Mouse, putting it on his head.
"Now I can see why you've been
so busy dreaming. It's my very
special Dream Hat!"

"We've both been very busy,"
said Little Mouse, yawning.
"There's just time to do one
more thing," said Big Mouse.

"And that's to have a nice
long snooze!" Big Mouse and Little Mouse
curled up together underneath the leaves.
Little Mouse's hat fell off, and Big
Mouse's hat slid right
down over his nose.